KING MIDAS
AND THE GOLDEN TOUCH

Retold by **FREYA LITTLEDALE**
From the tale by Nathaniel Hawthorne
Illustrated by **DANIEL HORNE**

SCHOLASTIC INC.
New York Toronto London Auckland Sydney

Once upon a time
there was a king named Midas
who loved gold more than
anything in the world.
But the more gold he had,
the more gold he wanted.
He lived in a splendid palace
with his little daughter, Marigold.

Every morning, Marigold went out to the rose garden
to pick flowers, chase butterflies,
and feed the birds.

And every morning, King Midas went to a secret room
beneath the palace where he kept his golden treasures.
He locked the door with his gold key
and often said to himself:

My garden is lovely, I've been told,
but not as lovely as solid gold.
Gardens don't twinkle.
Gardens don't shine.
They don't last forever like this gold of mine.

One morning, King Midas sat in his secret room,
building tiny towers with his gold coins.
Suddenly, the room grew bright.
Midas looked up and saw a stranger
standing in a golden light.
"Surely, this is a magical being," Midas thought.

"I know all about you, King Midas," said the stranger.
"And I have come to grant you a wish."

"Just one?" asked Midas.
King Midas thought about his garden.
What if all the roses turned to gold?
Then he would have a great garden of gold!
"I wish," said Midas, "that everything I touch
would turn to gold."

"Aha," said the stranger, "you want the Golden Touch!
Will it make you happy?"

"Yes! Yes!" cried Midas. "How could it fail?"

"Very well," said the stranger,
"tomorrow at sunrise your wish will come true."
Then the stranger disappeared.

Before sunrise, the next morning,
Midas touched his bedside table.
Nothing happened.
He touched a candle on the table.
Still, nothing happened.
King Midas felt very sorry for himself.
"Perhaps the stranger
was only in my dreams," he thought.

But then, as the first sunbeam
shone through the window,
his blanket turned to gold.
It was as fine as a spider's web.

"My wish has come true!" cried Midas.
"I have the Golden Touch!"

Midas was so happy, he leaped out of bed
and ran around the room.

He touched a footstool with his fingertips.
At once it changed to gold.
He picked up a book.
The cover turned to gold.
It was wonderful to see.
But when he opened the book,
all the words were gone.
Every page was a blank sheet of gold.

King Midas put on his clothes
and looked in the mirror.
"Amazing!" he thought.
The silk had changed to spun gold.
It felt just a little heavy,
but Midas didn't mind.

Then he picked up a handkerchief
Marigold had made for his birthday.
The handkerchief turned to gold.
Midas shook his head. "That's too bad," he said.

But when he put on his spectacles,
he couldn't see a thing.
Now the glass was solid gold.
"Oh, well," he told himself,
"spectacles don't matter.
I only need them to read."

Marigold was still asleep
when King Midas ran out to the garden.
The smell of roses filled the air.

One by one, he touched each bush,
and every flower turned to gold.
Even the bees and butterflies
on the petals became pure gold.

By now, Midas was very hungry,
so he rushed back to the palace
for breakfast.

Besides coffee and juice,
there were hot muffins, pancakes,
and fresh, ripe strawberries.
It looked so good,
Midas could hardly wait for Marigold.

Now, Marigold was a cheerful child
who almost never shed a tear.
But soon she came in crying.

"What is wrong?" asked Midas.

"Look at this rose!" she sobbed.

"It's beautiful!" said Midas.

"No, it's not! It's ugly," Marigold cried.
"All the roses in the garden are ugly.
 They're hard and cold,
 and they've lost their smell.
 What could have happened to them?"

"My sweet child," said Midas,
"you're too young to understand.
 That golden rose is worth more
 than any real flower.
 Now dry your eyes and eat your breakfast."

King Midas poured his coffee.
At once the pot turned to gold.
So did the cup and saucer.
"I'll have to build another room
to keep my new treasures safe," he thought.
"I'll start this very day."

Then Midas took a sip of coffee.
The instant the coffee touched his lips,
it turned to melted gold.
"Aaahhh!" he groaned.

"What's the matter?" asked Marigold.
She was eating a pancake
covered with butter and syrup.

"Nothing, dear," he told her.

Midas touched the stem of a strawberry.
Right before his eyes,
the juicy red fruit burst into pure gold —
stem and all.
It was very pretty.
But Midas was very, very hungry.
"I would give anything
for a real strawberry," he thought.

Midas didn't know what to do.
He leaned over the plate and grabbed a hot muffin
with his teeth.
But the Golden Touch was too fast for him.
Instead of a muffin, his mouth was full
of burning gold.
"Ohhhh!" King Midas yelled.

He jumped up from the table
and stomped around the dining hall.
"What's going to become of me?" he moaned.
"How could I have made such a wish?"

Marigold ran to him with tears in her eyes.
"Please, Father, please," she cried,
"tell me what is wrong!"

King Midas bent down and kissed her.
"My darling Marigold," he said,
"I've been so foolish."

But Marigold did not answer.
The moment he touched her, she changed.
Midas felt her little body grow stiff
in his arms.
Her brown curls turned gold.
Her eyes stared without seeing.
And the tears on her cheeks grew hard.
Marigold was no longer a living child,
but a golden statue.

"What have I done?" cried King Midas.
"With all my riches,
I am the poorest man on earth!"
And he fell to his knees and wept.

Just then, the hall shone with a golden light.
Midas looked up and saw the stranger.
"Well, King Midas," he asked, "are you happy now?"

"I am miserable," Midas answered.
"I have lost what I really loved."

"And what is that?" asked the stranger.

"I have lost my child," said Midas.

"You seem wiser today," said the stranger.
"Would you give up your Golden Touch?"

"I hate gold!" said Midas.

"Then go to the river near your palace
and bathe in the water," the stranger told him.
"Fill a pitcher with the same water
and sprinkle it over everything
you wish to change."

The stranger disappeared.
Midas lost no time.
He grabbed a clay pitcher
and trembled as it turned to gold.
Then he ran down the path to the river.

Into the water he jumped — clothes and all.
What a great splash he made!
In an instant, he felt lighter from head to toe.

As he filled the pitcher with water,
he watched it turn from gold to clay.
King Midas had never been so happy.
"At last," he thought,
"I've washed away the Golden Touch!"
But the sands of the river turned gold from his bath.
And they're gold to this very day.

Midas rushed back to the palace.
Quickly, he splashed water
over the golden statue of Marigold.
No sooner did the water fall on her
than the color returned to her cheeks.

"Please, Father, stop!" she cried.
"You're getting my dress all wet."

A glimmer of gold remained in Marigold's hair.
But she did not know she had been a golden statue.
She knew nothing about the Golden Touch.
And Midas did not tell her.

Outside in the garden, King Midas sprinkled water
over every golden bush.
The garden came back to life.
The bees buzzed.
The butterflies fluttered their wings.
And all the flowers bloomed.

Years later, when King Midas was a very old man,
Marigold's children sat in his lap
as he stroked their silken curls.
"Tell us a story, Grandpa," they said.

So Midas told them the story of his Golden Touch.

"Is that why you never wear a gold crown?" they asked.

"That's right, my little ones," he said.
"Ever since that day,
I've hated the sight of gold.
The only gold I love
is the gold in your hair."

To my mother
Dorothy

ISBN 0-590-42262-6

Text copyright © 1989 by Freya Littledale.
Illustrations copyright © 1989 by Daniel Horne.
All rights reserved. Published by Scholastic Inc.

12 11 10 9 8 7 6 5 4 3 2 1   9/8 0 1 2 3 4/9

Printed in the U.S.A.   23

First Scholastic printing, April 1989